آن شغالی رفت اندر خم رنگ

اندر آن خم کرد یک ساعت درنگ

tiny owl publishing

Text and Illustration Copyright © 2009 Nazar Publications
This edition © 2016 Tiny Owl Publishing Ltd
1 Repton House, Charlwood Street, SW1V 2LD, London, UK

Translated by Azita Rassi
Persian collection editor: Ali Seidabadi
Graphic designer: Elahe Javanmard

ISBN 978-1-910328-13-2

A catalogue record of this book is available from the British Library
www.tinyowl.co.uk

Tiny Owl Publishing Ltd,
Registered in England No. 08297587

The Jackal Who Thought He Was a Peacock

Firoozeh Golmohammadi

Peacock

A fable by Rumi

retold by Fereshteh Sarlak

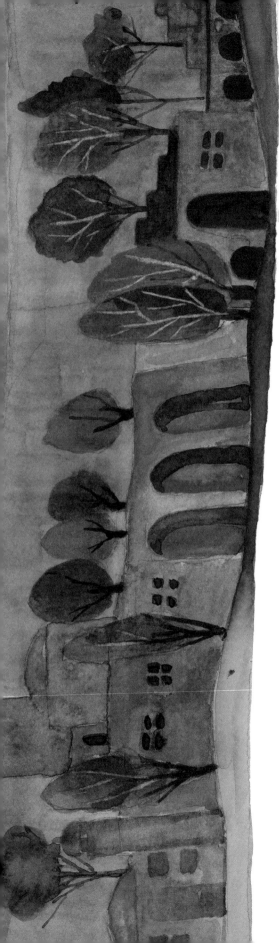

Once upon a time, in some far away land, lived a jackal. But this jackal was not happy being a jackal, with his brown and grey fur — he wanted to be bright like a peacock, with pretty, colourful feathers so that all animals would love and admire him.

Every time he found a colourful object, he put it on, thinking it would make him more like a peacock.

Each day he came out of his den and went over
to the peacocks' farm to watch the beautiful birds.
At dusk he returned to his den, rather sad and
tired, and with an even stronger desire to become
a peacock.

One night, the jackal dreamt that he had finally become a beautiful peacock and that all the animals were waiting on him hand and foot because of his great and brilliant beauty. He gave orders to the animals in the trees and on the land and they obeyed him.

Then he shouted so loudly in his dream that
he woke himself up. And he saw that he
was still just a plain brown and grey jackal.

He couldn't stop thinking about his dream and about how wonderful it had been to be a peacock. Then he had an idea: he went to the dyer's house.

The vats of paint at the dyer's house were all arranged in a row. They were shining brilliantly in the moonlight. The jackal jumped in each of them, one at a time, splashing about to get covered in the beautiful colours, and then leapt out again and went on his way home.

The dyer woke up when he heard the terrible racket and went to inspect the vats. He saw the painted trail of the jackal's paw prints and chased him all the way to his den. When he found him, he started shouting, saying that he'd stolen his valuable paints.

This commotion woke up the locals, who came out of their houses to find out what was happening. The sherrif asked what was going on.

The dyer told his story but the sheriff was still sleepy. He looked at the jackal and said, 'But this is a peacock.' Then he sent the dyer home before returning to his comfortable bed. The jackal, who now believed he had indeed become a peacock, relaxed and went on his way. He passed some of his jackal friends and told them that he was a peacock now. They thought he was crazy, but all he said was: 'I'm not a jackal. I'm a peacock!'

For breakfast, he decided to eat fruit, like all peacocks. But the more he examined the fruit, the less he liked the look of it. So he secretly went inside his den to eat tasty jackal food so nobody could see.

After he had finished eating, he went outside for his big performance. He wanted to convince everybody that he was a peacock by climbing a tree and gliding slowly down to the ground. But who has ever seen a flying jackal? He fell down suddenly and hurt himself all over.

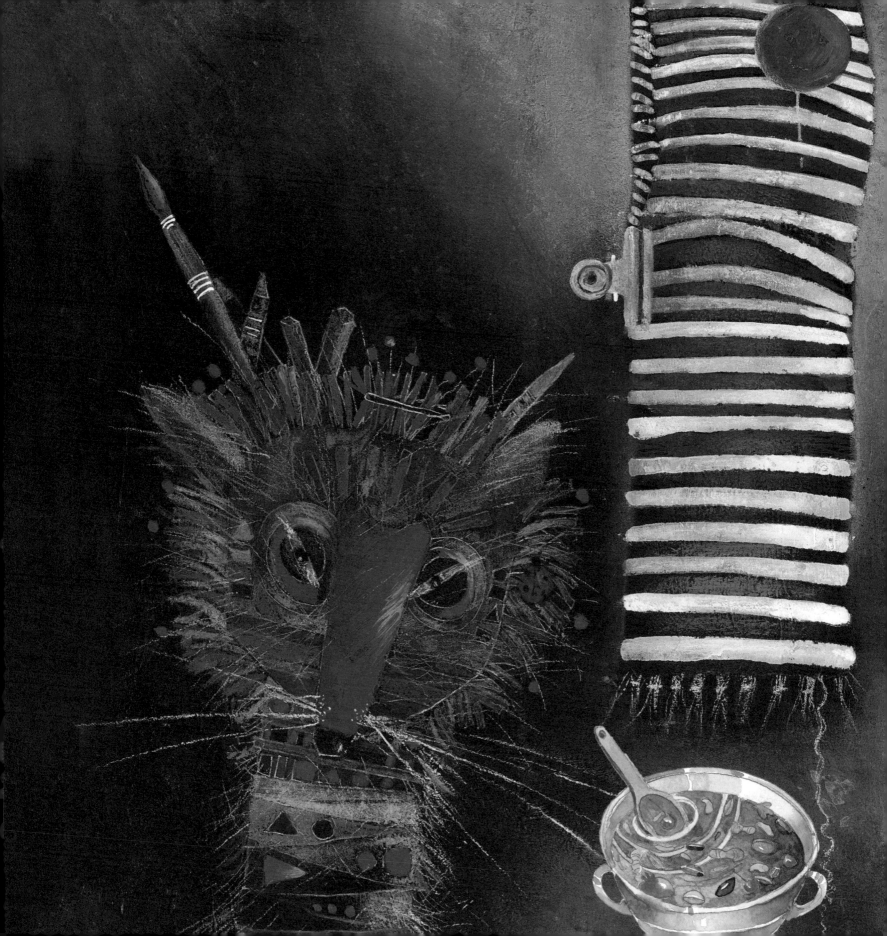

The poor jackal couldn't get up so his jackal friends helped and gently took him to his den, saying, 'Dear friend, paints won't make a peacock out of a jackal.'

The jackal decided to wash in the river and saw the beautiful colours disappear away with the current.

He still dreams today of becoming a peacock but whenever he thinks about how to do it, his body strangely starts to ache again, as if he's just fallen out of the tree.

In the meantime, he eats tasty jackal food. He still goes to the peacocks' farm, but perhaps a little less often, especially when he's called back by his friends for some jackal game.

About Rumi

This story is a rewriting of one of the fables in the prominent book of *Masnavi* by Rumi, the great 13th-century Persian mystic and poet. We believe that Rumi is a poet of the whole world and everybody can read and enjoy his works.

All of his works are gathered in two big collections. There is *Divan-e Shams,* which comprises his exhilarating sonnets, combining romantic and mystic passion with lively music. His devotees dance the Sema while singing these sonnets. Rumi's other outstanding book is *Masnavi,* which explains philosophical and mystical concepts through beautiful, metaphorical allegories containing mystical points as well as wisdom and advice.

In her rewriting of *The Jackal Who Thought He Was a Peacock,* Fereshteh Sarlak has tried to bring the allegory closer to children's lives by expanding the story.

About the illustrator

Firoozeh Golmohammadi, the Iranian artist and illustrator born in 1951, is known as an artist who revolutionised Persian miniature paintings. She has also used miniature techniques in her illustrations and has achieved a personal style, so that her works attract both the attention of the general public and that of artistic festivals.

Her works have been exhibited in various countries in Europe, America, the Middle East and the Far East. Her illustrations have been admitted to different biennales and have won more than 15 reputable international awards.

Among Rumi's works, his *The Parrot and the Merchant* has been published by Tiny Owl, retold and illustrated by Marjan Vafaian.

پس برآمد پوستش زنگین شده

که منم طاووس علیین شده